the pain
and
the great one

Books by Judy Blume

YOUNG ADULT AND MIDDLE GRADE

Are You There God? It's Me, Margaret.

Blubber

Deenie

Forever . . .

Here's to You, Rachel Robinson

Iggie's House

It's Not the End of the World

Just as Long as We're Together

Letters to Judy: What Kids Wish They Could Tell You

Places I Never Meant to Be: Original Stories by Censored Writers
(edited by Judy Blume)

Starring Sally J. Freedman as Herself

Then Again, Maybe I Won't

Tiger Eyes

THE FUDGE BOOKS

Tales of a Fourth Grade Nothing

Otherwise Known as Sheila the Great

Superfudge

Fudge-a-mania

Double Fudge

PICTURE BOOKS AND STORYBOOKS

The One in the Middle Is the Green Kangaroo

Freckle Juice

The Pain and the Great One series

Soupy Saturdays

Cool Zone

Going, Going, Gone!

Friend or Fiend?

JUDY BLUME

illustrations by Debbie Ridpath Ohi

the pain
and
the great one

A Richard Jackson Book
Atheneum Books for Young Readers
New York London Toronto Sydney New Delhi

ATHENEUM BOOKS FOR YOUNG READERS
An imprint of Simon & Schuster Children's Publishing Division
1230 Avenue of the Americas, New York, New York 10020
ATHENEUM BOOKS FOR YOUNG READERS is a registered
trademark of Simon & Schuster, Inc.
Atheneum logo is a trademark of Simon & Schuster, Inc.
For information about special discounts for bulk purchases, please contact Simon &
Schuster Special Sales at 1-866-506-1949 or business@simonandschuster.com.
The Simon & Schuster Speakers Bureau can bring authors to your live event.
For more information or to book an event, contact the
Simon & Schuster Speakers Bureau
at 1-866-248-3049 or visit our website at www.simonspeakers.com.
Also available in an Atheneum Books for Young Readers paperback edition
Book design by Tom Daly
The text for this book is set in New Century Schoolbook LT Std.
The illustrations for this book are digitally rendered.
Manufactured in the United States of America
1017 PCH
This Atheneum Books for Young Readers hardcover edition May 2014
2 4 6 8 10 9 7 5 3
Library of Congress Cataloging-in-Publication Data
Blume, Judy.
The Pain and the Great One / Judy Blume ; illustrated by Debbie Ridpath Ohi.
pages cm
"A Richard Jackson Book."
Originally published in a slightly different form by Bradbury Press in 1974.
Summary: A six-year-old (The Pain) and his eight-year-old sister (The Great One) see
each other as troublemakers and the best-loved in the family.
ISBN 978-1-4814-1146-2 (hardcover)
ISBN 978-1-4814-1145-5 (paperback)
[1. Brothers and sisters—Fiction. 2. Sibling rivalry—Fiction.] I. Ohi, Debbie Ridpath,
1962– illustrator. II. Title.
PZ7.B6265Pai 2014
[E]—dc23   2014007151

This title was previously published in a slightly different form.

To the original Pain and the Great One with Love
—J. B.

For Ruth, the best sister in the world
—D. R. O.

The Pain

My brother's a pain.
He won't get out of bed
In the morning.
Mom has to carry him
Into the kitchen.
He opens his eyes
When he smells
His cornflakes.

He should get dressed himself.
He's six.
He's in first grade.
But he's so pokey
Daddy has to help him
Or he'd never be ready in time
And he'd miss the bus.

He cries if I
Leave without him.
Then Mom gets mad
And yells at me
Which is another reason why
My brother's a pain.

He's got to be first
To show Mom
His schoolwork.
She says *ooh* and *aah*
Over all his pictures
Which aren't great at all
But just ordinary
First grade stuff.

At dinner he picks
At his food.
He's not supposed
To get dessert
If he doesn't
Eat his meat.
But he always
Gets it anyway.

When he takes a bath
My brother the pain
Powders the whole bathroom
And never gets his face clean.
Daddy says
He's learning to
Take care of himself.
I say,
He's a slob!

The Pain and the Great One

My brother the Pain
Is two years younger than me.
So how come
He gets to stay up
As late as I do?
Which isn't really late enough
For somebody in third grade
Anyway.
I asked Mom and Daddy about that.
They said,
"You're right.
You *are* older.
You *should* stay up later."

So they tucked the Pain
Into bed.
I couldn't wait
For the fun to begin.
I waited
And waited
And waited.
But Daddy and Mom
Just sat there
Reading books.

Finally I shouted,
"I'm going to bed!"

"We thought you wanted
To stay up later,"
They said.

"I did.
But without the Pain
There's nothing to do!"

"Remember that tomorrow,"
Mom said.
And she smiled.

But the next day
My brother was a pain again.
When I got a phone call
He danced all around me
Singing stupid songs
At the top of his lungs.
Why does he have to act that way?

And why does he always
Want to be garbage man
When I build a city
Out of blocks?
Who needs him
Knocking down buildings
With his dumb old trucks!

And I would really like to know
Why the cat sleeps on the Pain's bed
Instead of mine
Especially since I am the one
Who feeds her.
That is the meanest thing of all!

The Pain and the Great One

I don't understand
How Mom can say
The Pain is lovable.
She's always kissing him
And hugging him
And doing disgusting things
Like that.
And Daddy says
The Pain is just what
They always wanted.

YUCK!

I think they love him better than me.

The Great One

My sister thinks she's so great
Just because she's older
Which makes Daddy and Mom think
She's really smart.
But I know the truth.
My sister's a jerk.

She thinks she's great
Just because she can
Play the piano
And you can tell
The songs are real ones.
But I like my songs better
Even if nobody
Ever heard them before.

My sister thinks she's so great
Just because she can work
The can opener.
Which means she gets
To feed the cat.
Which means the cat
Likes her better than me
Just because she feeds her.

My sister thinks she's so great
Just because Aunt Diana lets
Her watch the baby
And tells her how much
The baby likes *her.*

And all the time
The baby is sleeping
In my dresser drawer.
Which Mom has fixed up
Like a bed
For when the baby
Comes to visit.
And I'm not supposed
To touch him
Even if he's
In *my* drawer
And gets changed
On *my* bed.

My sister thinks she's so great
Just because she can
Remember phone numbers.
And when she dials
She never gets
The wrong person.

And when she has friends over
They build whole cities
Out of blocks.
I like to be garbage man.
I zoom my trucks all around.

So what if I knock down
Some of their buildings?

"It's not fair
That she always gets
To use the blocks!"
I told Daddy and Mom.
They said,
"You're right.
Today you can use the blocks
All by yourself."
"I'm going to build a whole city
Without you!"
I told the Great One.

"Go ahead," she said.
"Go build a whole state without me.
See if I care!"

So I did.
I built a whole country
All by myself.
Only it's not the funnest thing
To play blocks alone.
Because when I zoomed my trucks
And knocked down buildings
Nobody cared but me!

"Remember that tomorrow,"
Mom said, when I told her
I was through playing blocks.

But the next day
We went swimming.
I can't stand my sister
When we go swimming.
She thinks she's so great
Just because she can swim and dive
And isn't afraid
To put her face
In the water.

I'm scared to put mine in
So she calls me *baby*.

Which is why
I have to
Spit water at her
And pull her hair
And even pinch her sometimes.

And I don't think it's fair
For Daddy and Mom to yell at me
Because none of it's my fault.
But they yell anyway.

Then Mom hugs my sister
And messes with her hair
And does other disgusting things
Like that.
And Daddy says
The Great One is just what
They always wanted.

YUCK!

I think they
love her better
than me.

JUDY BLUME, one of America's most popular authors, is the recipient of the 2004 National Book Foundation's Medal for Distinguished Contribution to American Letters. She is the #1 *New York Times* bestselling author of many beloved books for young people, including *Freckle Juice* and *The One in the Middle Is the Green Kangaroo*. Her work has been translated into thirty-two languages. Visit Judy at JudyBlume.com or follow her on Twitter @JudyBlume.